When You Wish Upon a Star

PERFORMED BY **Judy Collins**   PAINTINGS BY **Eric Puybaret**

MUSIC BY **Ned Washington**   LYRICS BY **Leigh Harline**

imagine!
a Peter Yarrow Book

When a star is born,
They possess a gift or two,
One of them is this
They have the power
To make a wish come true.

When you wish upon a star,
Makes no diff'rence who you are,

Anything your heart desires
will come to you.

If your heart is in your dream,
No request is too extreme,

When you wish upon a star as dreamers do.

Fate is kind,
She brings to those who love,
The sweet fulfillment
of their secret longing.

Like a bolt out of the blue,
Fate steps in and sees you thru,

When you wish upon a star
Your dream comes true.

Fate is kind,
She brings to those who love,
The sweet fulfillment
of their secret longing.

Like a bolt out of the blue,
Fate steps in and sees you thru,

When you wish upon a star
Your dream comes true.

~ Performer's Note ~

In all my years of singing great songs, I have seldom found one that matched "When You Wish Upon a Star" for inspiration, beauty of melody and phrasing, and timeless impact. The song has traveled with many of us through generations, through our childhoods and into the coming true of some of our most important dreams and wishes—wishes for peace, for joy, for love, and for happiness in our lives. In singing it for you now, I find a renewed belief in all the things the song promises—for hope, above all. As I sing the song, I wish you renewed belief in your very special dreams. May they all come true.

~Judy Collins

~ Illustrator's Note ~

Reading the words of this wonderful song, the question that came to mind was: How do I transcribe the abstract subject of hope into pictures? Meeting the Star, all of us would have such different wishes. What kind of painting could express a universal form of desire? This is what I thought about while drawing all these children and fairies. It was an exciting challenge!

~Eric Puybaret

I dedicate my performance of "When You Wish Upon a Star" to my mother, Marjorie;

January 1916–Dec 2010, and my father, Charles, April 1911–May 1968;

With love and gratitude for their love of art and beauty and the appreciation of wonderful songs

that they brought into my life. –Judy Collins —Singer, Writer, Activist

for Joséphine. –Eric

Library of Congress Cataloging-in-Publication Data
Washington, Ned, 1901–1976.
When you wish upon a star / lyrics by Ned Washington ; music by Leigh Harline ; paintings by Eric Puybaret ; performed by Judy Collins.
p. cm.
"An Imagine book"--T.p. verso.
Summary: The paintings of Eric Puybaret illustrate the words of the song from Walt Disney's film, Pinocchio.
ISBN-13: 978-1-936140-35-0   ISBN-10: 1-936140-35-7
1. Children's songs, English--United States--Texts. [1. Wishes--Songs and music.
2. Songs.] I. Harline, Leigh. II. Puybaret, Eric, ill. III. Collins, Judy. IV. Title.
PZ8.3.W247Wk 2011 782.42--dc22 [E]
2011004945
1 3 5 7 9 10 8 6 4 2

An Imagine Book Published by Charlesbridge
85 Main Street Watertown, MA 02472
617-926-0329 www.charlesbridge.com

Printed in China
Manufactured in June 2011
ISBN 13: 978-1-936140-35-0

For information about custom editions, special sales, premium and corporate purchases,
please contact Charlesbridge Publishing, Inc. at specialsales@charlesbridge.com

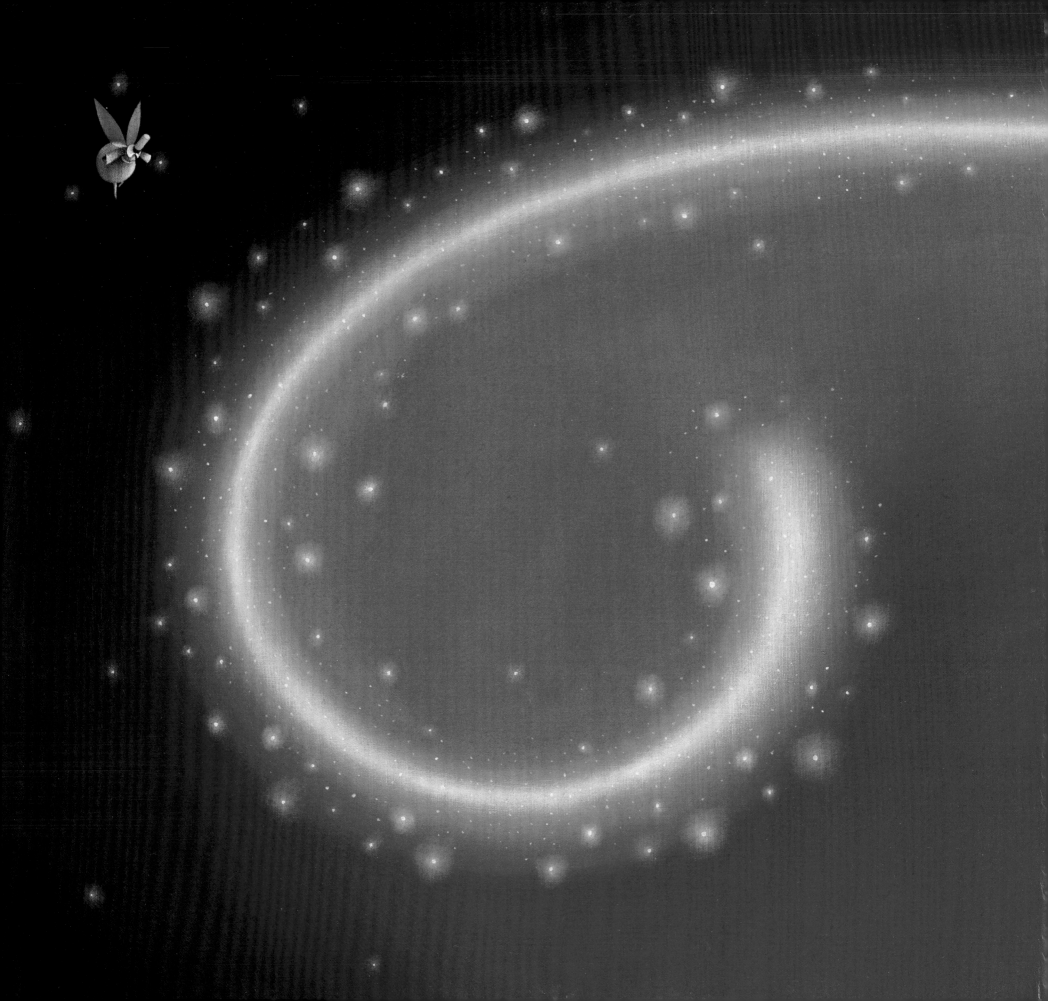